Little Kids Do **BIG** Things

BIG
SHAGGY MAX

Patricia T. Tanenbaum and Carol A. Zaslow

Archway Publishing books may be ordered through booksellers or by contacting:

Archway Publishing
1663 Liberty Drive
Bloomington, IN 47403
www.archwaypublishing.com
1 (888) 242-5904

ISBN: 978-1-4808-6021-6 (sc)
ISBN: 978-1-4808-6020-9 (e)

Print information available on the last page.

Archway Publishing rev. date: 06/05/2018

For those most precious—our families,
children—champion problem solvers,
animal lovers everywhere.

And Debra Mostow Zakarin, our forever cheerleader—P.T.T. and C.A.Z.

A portion of sales will be donated to the Delta Rescue Sanctuary—loving home
to more than 1,500 abandoned cats and dogs rescued from the wilderness.

"No!" gasp Alex and Oliver as they hear a loud CRASH and see black pieces of porcelain scattered all over.

Alex and his best friend, Oliver, love to have fun, but trouble seems to follow and this day is no different. As they play pinball bowling down the Bigsbys' long hallway, the yellow baseball suddenly slams right into Alex's parents' very tall and very fancy-dancy vase.

Grammy comes running. "NOW, look what you've done! Your mom told you to play outside. Does this hall look like a bowling alley?"

"Grammy, I'm sorry," says Alex, picking up the pieces very carefully.

"How did THAT happen?" asks Oliver.

"I don't know," says Alex, shaking his head back and forth. "I really don't know."

"Hey, Alex," says Oliver. "Let's make Mac!"

"Just maybe this cold, slimy, clammy goo will help us put the vase back together again," Alex says as he stirs the goo to make Mac. "I am mad. I was gonna ask my mom and dad if I can get a dog." Alex stirs even harder. "Again. I was going to ask them again."

"Bad timing," Oliver says.

Suddenly, Alex jumps when he hears "I'm home!" He doesn't remember his mom having such a loud voice.

"MOM!" Alex practically shouts.

Mrs. Bigsby looks at Alex and Oliver. They are covered in the gooey Mac ingredients as are the counter and the floor.

"Clean this up immediately," Mrs. Bigsby says as she storms out of the kitchen.

"Just wait till she finds out about the vase," moans Alex.

"Good morning, class," says Mrs. Rose with a wide smile. "Who would like to be the first one to share today?" she asks as she writes "Sharing Time" in big letters on the board.

Ella, the friendliest girl in the third grade, shows off her painted fingernails. "Grandma and I had manicures!" she proudly announces.

Toby brags about how he won a big goldfish at some fair.

Alex can't wait any longer. "I need help," he blurts out and goes on to explain how he means to do the right thing but somehow always gets into trouble. "And then," Alex finishes his story, "my parents say I'm not responsible enough to take care of a dog, and I have wanted a dog for so long. I even dream about it."

Hands shoot up. Mrs. Rose points to Ella, who sits up straight and brushes the hair out of her eyes.

"You can volunteer at Mr. Peaches' Pooches. You know…that pet store with all those super cute dogs he rescues from the pound."

"Good idea, Ella," Mrs. Rose says. "And, Alex, I'm sure you would learn a lot about caring for a dog."

Alex opens the big red door to Mr. Peaches' Pooches. He tries not to breathe in the gross smell that reminds him of his dad's vitamins.

From behind an old-fashioned cash register that makes the sound *ca-ching! ca-ching!* and a drawer that pops open, Mr. Peaches yells, "Welcome, Alex Bigsby!" His cheeks are rosy red, and he wears a baseball cap that covers his bald head.

"Thanks," Alex replies. He feels he is going to like it at Mr. Peaches' Pooches.

"Meet the pups," Mr. Peaches proudly remarks, showing Alex around.

Lucy is curled up in a little furry ball. And Cupcake wags her tail when they stop at her pen. Mr. Peaches gives her a little love pat and she barks.

"She says, *thank you*," Alex says with a laugh.

Ruff! Ruff! comes from the oversized pen in the back.

"I hear you, Max," chuckles Mr. Peaches.

Alex gasps! "Mr. Peaches, that dog looks like the dog I dream about."

He plops down on the floor right in front of the big hairy dog and begins petting him.

Max instantly begins licking Alex. His tail wags back and forth.

"Looks like you have a new friend," Mr. Peaches says as he slightly lifts his baseball cap and wipes the sweat from his brow. "Max is a big dog. He needs a lot of brushing and exercise."

"I can do that!" Alex says, jumping to his feet. "How does Max see with his hair falling over his eyes?"

"Oh, he does fine," explains Mr. Peaches. "Actually, that long hair protects his eyes, which are sensitive to the sun."

Alex smiles at Max and he could swear Max smiles back.

"Let's go for a walk," says Mr. Peaches. "You take Lucy and I'll take Max."

Max is a bundle of energy. As soon as they reach the park and are off leash, Max tramples the yellow daisies and makes a dash for the sprinklers. Darting in and out of the spray of water, he manages to get soaking wet.

Lucy yaps. Alex scoops her up. Her curls are a big wet mess.

After what seems like forever to drag Max back to the store, Mr. Peaches begins to laugh. "Those sprinklers are always a surprise."

Alex grabs a big towel and gently dries Max. Max looks into his eyes and licks his face.

"You're welcome," Alex whispers as he pulls Max close.

The next time Alex works at Mr. Peaches' Pooches, they try to teach Max some basic commands.

"Max, stay!" Mr. Peaches gently commands as he slowly backs away from him. Max sits very still staring at the treat Alex is holding.

"Come," Mr. Peaches says, snapping his fingers. Max runs for his treat.

"Max, stay!" Alex repeats when it's his turn. He shows Max a small treat. Then he backs away.

"Stay, stay," Alex repeats. But Max doesn't listen. He runs off.

Over and over again, they practice the "stay" and "come" commands. Just when Alex is about to give up Max finally obeys, coming only when Alex calls him.

"Good boy," Alex says. "Good boy."

One day Alex brings Oliver to Mr. Peaches' Pooches. They head straight to the biggest cage in the back.

Woof, woof, Max barks.

"Sit, big boy." When Max sits, Alex gives him a treat.

Alex and Oliver sit inside of Max's pen and take turns brushing him.

"Stay," Alex says to Max.

He gets up to refill the water bowl and forgets to close the gate. Max races out and knocks over a huge display of canned dog food.

CRASH! A rack holding brightly colored leashes and collars is strewn across the floor, scattered in all directions.

Alex drops the water bowl as Max crashes into him and immediately begins licking him. The bowl shatters.

Oliver says, "Here we go again! Where's the Mac?"

"It's my fault, Mr. Peaches," Alex quickly explains, eyeing the puddle of water on the floor. "I forgot to close the pen gate. I won't do that again. Ever. I promise."

"Oh, Alex, what am I going to do with you?" Mr. Peaches says. "You arrived late twice this week and now this mess."

"I'm sorry, Mr. Peaches," Alex whispers. "I really am."

"Accidents happen," he says with a long sigh. "I know you're trying your best."

A few days later, their pockets stuffed with dog treats, Alex and Oliver grab their backpacks and bikes and speed off. They pass the Book Mart and Luigi's Pizza and stop at Gil's General Store for some lemonade from Gil's fake lemon tree. Then, Alex and Oliver head over to Mr. Peaches' Pooches to surprise Mr Peaches.

The door jingles open. "Greetings, boys! What a pleasant surprise!" exclaims Mr. Peaches, who is on the floor with Cupcake.

"We're back!" says Alex with a smile.

"Happy to have you," says Mr. Peaches.

Alex and Oliver fill their pockets with more treats and gently approach a newcomer, a little black dog named Night.

"Where's Max?" Oliver asks as Alex points to the empty pen.

"He's probably outside getting groomed. You know how tangled his shaggy hair gets," Alex says with more confidence than he feels.

In a split second, they run out the back door and holler his name. "Max! Max! Max!" They run back inside.

"Mr. Peaches!" Alex practically shouts. "We can't find Max. Where is he?" Alex feels like he wants to throw up.

"Great news!" Mr. Peaches says. "A lovely couple adopted Max and took him home yesterday."

"What?" Alex can hardly believe his ears. He begins to feel hot and his stomach tightens. Tears start to form. He gulps hard to hold them back.

"I love Max," he blurts.

Alex can't believe it. Max is his. He feels like Max belongs to him.

"Max is a rescue dog," Mr. Peaches gently explains. "We need to be happy for him. Now he has a permanent home."

Alex hardly hears Mr. Peaches. "No. No. No," Alex says over and over again.

"Max will be well loved by two people who will shower him with attention. He will help them, too, and provide great energy and spirit. They are older and have the time to give him the kind of home he needs." Mr. Peaches pauses for a moment. "There'll be other dogs—you'll see."

"Max is gone! An older couple has taken him home," Alex says as he slams the door behind him. "It's not fair."

His mom turns and sees Alex's teary eyes. His dad looks up from the newspaper.

"I know this doesn't seem fair," his dad says, handing him a tissue. "We're so proud of the job you're doing. You're working hard to arrive on time and you haven't missed a week. Remember, it's Mr. Peaches' job to find the dogs good homes. Max finally has space and a loving home."

"I know I should be happy for him, but I'm so sad. It's not fair. Max was supposed to be MY dog!"

At school the next day, "COMMUNITY" is scrawled across the board.

"What people and places make up our community?" asks Mrs. Rose.

The class talks about firefighters, police officers, postal workers, and teachers.

"What about Mr. Peaches?" asks Oliver. "He is the nicest guy and he does pet adoptions."

"He provides a valuable service to our community," adds Ella.

Alex points to the class motto hanging above the board—Little Kids Do BIG Things. "I have a big thing we can do," he says with a smile.

The kids get to work. There is a lot of planning for a Pet Adoption Day with Mr. Peaches' Pooches.

On the big day, the Bigsbys, Grammy, and Grandpa Joe arrive early. But already the grassy playground is bustling.

"Grandpa, let's get hot dogs for lunch," Alex says as he points to the fire engine red booth.

Yellow, blue, and green canvas booths are set up, and customers buy lemonade and cotton candy. Loud music blasts from speakers. In the middle of the playground are large steel pens filled with big and little dogs.

Alex looks at all the dogs and hopes they all find their forever home today. He sees his best friend and shouts, "Hey, Oliver, let's say hi to Mr. Peaches!"

Oliver nods as he takes a bite out of his corn on the cob.

Some of the smaller dogs are running around in circles. Ella is leaning over, trying to pet Cupcake.

"Alex, Ella is adopting Cupcake," announces Mr. Peaches with a great big grin.

"That's great," Alex says. "Do you need help?"

"No, but there are some people by the oak tree who want to meet you," says Mr. Peaches, pointing. "Go have a look."

Alex walks toward the trees where an older couple is sitting on a green wooden bench. Next to them is a big, shaggy-haired gray-and-white English sheepdog.

As Alex moves closer, his heart begins to race.

Max begins to bark. He jumps up and nearly picks up the bench, where his leash is tied.

Alex grabs Max and hugs him so tightly. Max begins furiously licking Alex's face. "Wait!" Alex asks confused, "Why is Max here?"

"We want you to have him," the older man says. "My wife and I adopted Max. He's a friendly, playful dog and we tried our best to make a home for him, but Max has too much energy for us. He needs to go on long walks, to play ball at the park, and do all the things kids enjoy."

Alex is too busy hugging Max and isn't really paying attention.

The older man continues, "Mr. Peaches called your parents, and we planned this surprise. He told us you were brokenhearted and how hard you've been working. This decision was easy," the man says, smiling broadly.

"You mean that Max can be MY dog and live at MY house? I thought I would never see Max again!"

"Meet Max, MY VERY OWN DOG!" Alex exclaims.

"Max is one lucky dog," says Mrs. Rose. "Pet Adoption Day is bringing love and joy to many families. Just as our class motto says . . . "

"Little Kids Do BIG Things," the kids say all together.

"*Ruff! Ruff! Ruff!*" Max barks loudly.

Alex and Oliver's Mac Recipe

Please note: Do not prepare Mac on your own. Prepare only with **Adult Supervision**. **Be sure not to eat it.** *Have fun!*

Materials

8 oz. Elmer's® white glue
Borax (a common household cleaner)
large mixing bowl
warm water
old spoon

yellow food coloring
measuring cup
plastic cup (8 oz. size works well)
zipper-lock bag (so it won't dry out too fast!)
paper towels (clean-up is essential!)

Directions

1. Empty the glue into the mixing bowl.

2. Fill the empty glue bottle with warm water. Screw on the cap tightly and shake.

3. Pour the water from the bottle into the mixing bowl, and use the spoon to mix well with the glue.

4. Add a drop or two of food coloring.

5. Measure ½ cup of warm water into the plastic cup.

6. Add one teaspoon of Borax to the water in the cup and stir. Don't worry if the powder dissolves. *This solution is the secret linking agent that causes the glue molecules to become Mac.*

7. Stirring the glue in the mixing bowl, slowly add a little of the Borax solution. Immediately, you will feel the long strands of molecules start to connect.

8. It's time to abandon the spoon and use your hands to do the serious mixing. Keep adding the Borax solution to the glue mixture (but don't stop mixing) until it's the consistency you want. You might like your Mac stringy. Others might like it firm. You're the boss—it's all yours. You're going to love this!

9. After playing, store the Mac in a zipper-lock bag so it keeps. Then it's cleanup time—with the paper towels.

PATRICIA T. TANENBAUM taught at a private school in New York City, raised three children, and founded the Beverly Hills Unified K-12 Community Service Learning Program. **CAROL A. ZASLOW,** mother of two, taught early education in Inglewood, California, and as PTA president developed the Community Service Program at her daughters' school. Together, they developed a popular annual fundraiser in California, *Kids Helping Kids For Literacy* Scrabble Challenge. For more information about the authors and to have them visit your school, please go to PAZAZZ! www.pzzcares.com

9 781480 860216